DREAMS OF THE DEFEATED

A Play in Two Acts

by

Joel D. Hirst

Joel D. Hirst

<u>Cast of Characters</u>

<u>Prisoner</u>: A young man just entering adulthood, not an adolescent but not yet a man. Leader of the September Seventh rebellion.

<u>Voice</u>: A guide, a guardian, maybe a mentor.

<u>Judge</u>: In her sixties, she is the judge, jury and potential executioner; she is responsible for implementing The Elders' will through the Perfect Order.

<u>Accuser</u>: A young woman working for the state. It is unclear where she gets the right to challenge the prisoner, as she remains anonymous throughout.

<u>Witness</u>: A young man, one of the leaders of the breakaway movement within September Seventh, who is now working for the state.

<u>Warden</u>: A man in his fifties, warden for the prison where the prisoner had spent time awaiting trial.

<u>Scene</u>
The prison and the courtroom, in the capital city.

<u>Time</u>
Yesterday, today, and tomorrow.

Dreams of the Defeated

ACT I

Scene 1

SETTING: An underground jail cell. It is dark, almost pitch black. In the corner of the cell is a dirty toilet without a lid and a constantly dripping faucet. Refuse is piled up close to the entrance, with rats and roaches crawling through it. Three bars seal off a small high window, painted black but with light emanating from cracks in the black paint and around the edges. Rusted bars mark the entrance to the cell, with a large padlock and chains. A single wire hangs over the cell, with the light bulb removed.

AT RISE: Light escaping through the cracks in the painted-over window shines upon the face of the prisoner, gaunt and streaked with grime. He is an adolescent or young adult, is Caucasian with disheveled blond hair over a five-o'clock shadow. He is wearing a tattered black and white checkered prison outfit, without shoes. He is lying in the fetal position on an old brown mattress, with no blanket or pillow.

VOICE

 (off)
You know you're never going to get out of here.
 (A booming, powerful, convincing voice.)

                    PRISONER
         (Sitting up from the supine position on
         the mattress, alarmed.)
What, what's that? Who's there?

                     VOICE
         (off)
You don't know me, but I've been watching you.

                    PRISONER
         (Unbending, his knees popping and his
         back creaking, he stands and
         inadvertently brushes the live wire with
         his ear and receives a jolt. He cringes
         and puts his hand to his ear.)
God?
         (hopeful)

                     VOICE
         (off)
No, you idiot.
         (The deep radiating voice chortles.)

                    PRISONER
The devil—
         (More alarmed.)

                     VOICE
         (off)

         (Cutting him off.)
Nothing that sinister.

                    PRISONER
Then who, who are you and what do you want?
         (befuddled)

                    VOICE
          (off)
Want? What makes you think I want anything?
And what makes you think you could give it to
me, assuming I did?

                  PRISONER
Huh? What's that supposed to… It's just err…
Huh?
          (more confusion)

                    VOICE
          (off)
Nice speech. You came here with quite a
reputation as a wordsmith. Cat got your
tongue?
          (a brief delay)
Well?

                  PRISONER
          (Starting to get angry.)
Who the hell *are* you? What do you want? You
know, never mind, I don't care. I don't have
to answer to *you*.
          (Recovering from confusion, becoming
          angry with feigned outrage.)

                    VOICE
          (off)
How do you know? You don't know me.

                  PRISONER
          (Puffing out his chest, aggressive.)
Tell me who you are then!

                         VOICE
          (off)
Never!
          (In mocking defiance, the guttural
          chuckle clangs around the empty cell.)

          (silence)

          (The cord somewhere to the left of the
          prisoner's head sets off a silver-white
          spark. In the darkness something
          scuttles; causing the *plank* of an
          unbalanced spoon as it slides off a metal
          tray. Plunk, plunk, plunk - the constant
          dripping of the faucet beside the open
          toilet counts off the time. The prisoner
          slowly deflates, looking around for
          something else to focus on.)
You're never gonna get out of here.

                       PRISONER
Stop saying that! My being here has a purpose.
          (His voice comes out too shrill for the
          confidence he is seeking.)

                         VOICE
          (off)
That's what you think. That's what they all
said.
          (For a moment losing its scorn.)

                       PRISONER
Who all?

                    VOICE
          (off)
You think you are the first to come here? You
think you're the only one to get caught? Tsk
tsk.
          (pity)
Oh, but I can tell you stories. Once—

                  PRISONER
I don't need your stories.
          (Haughty and attempting to project
          bravado.)

                    VOICE
          (off)
Are you sure? You may learn something.

                  PRISONER
From you?
          (incredulous)
Whoever the hell you are, harassing prisoners
in the dark, who won't even show himself. *I*
learn from *you*? Damn you, Coward.

                    VOICE
          (off)
Bite me, jackass.
          (More cackling laughter.)

          (A moment's silence again.)
So this is how you converse, name calling?
You're less than I thought.

                  PRISONER
I'm more than you can conceive.

                    VOICE
          (off)
Than **I** can conceive?
          (Emphasis on the I.)
Tsk, tsk, tsk. Like I said, stick around, you
might come to change your mind. Oh, wait,
you're not going anywhere, are you?
          (chuckling)
Just what I like, a captive audience.
          (Stretching the word captive, making it
          sinister.)

                    PRISONER
          (indignant, arrogant)
Change my mind? Without even knowing you, I
still say with confidence that I already know
more than you can even imagine. That's why I'm
here.

                    VOICE
          (off)
Or, or. You're here because you know nothing.

                    PRISONER
          (Interrupting the voice, the retort is
          quiet.)
I know my destiny.
          (Voice betraying doubt.)

                    VOICE
          (off)
Wow, *destiny.*
          (The word dripping.)
Shit, I've never heard that before. Never
mind, I must be wrong. You may proceed to
ignore me.

                    PRISONER
I wish I could.
          (The prisoner mumbles, and shrugs while
          gesturing around the room.)

                     VOICE
          (off)

(A pounding laugh.)

                    PRISONER
What do you want with me anyway?
          (Walking over in the direction of the
          voice, straining, eyes squinting as he
          tries to look in the direction of the
          voice.)

                     VOICE
          (off)
Ever considered I'm just as bored as you; that
while your struggle gets old, so does mine?

                    PRISONER
So I'm your entertainment while you wait? You
think you're the first to have fun with me?
I've seen it all, in here all this time. So
trust me when I say that you aren't even
mildly intimidating, or interesting. After
you've been through what I've been through. So
you know what, just leave me alone!
          (His arm flails wildly.)

VOICE
     (off)
It might not be exactly how you think.
     (The voice whispers, almost apologetic.)

PRISONER
Aha, so you're a prisoner too? Were you told
by the guards to taunt me for an extra biscuit
at dinner? Does making fun of me buy you a
moment away from the torture? Or does mocking
me soothe a heart dark and cold? Or maybe
you're just a plain, ordinary mocker, poking
fun at me from the darkness.

VOICE
     (off)
The latter, of course. But who wouldn't?
     (Sarcastic. Scoffing. Back in charge.)
Look at you - you make it easy, all that
destiny talk from beside a stinking toilet.
You're not exactly a hard mark.
     (A moment's wait.)
Come on, I'm kidding. Why so somber? OK, I'll
give. I'm not a prisoner - at least not in the
way that you think. That is to say, I'm not
imprisoned. And yes, I'm here for you, or more
specifically because of you, but also not as
you might imagine.

PRISONER
What was your crime?

VOICE
     (off)
What makes you think I committed a crime?
Maybe it was just a failure.

                    PRISONER
Oh, so you're like me - innocent?

                     VOICE
          (off)
Ja!
          (Then, more softly.)
Sorry. That just slipped out. You're thinking
about this the wrong way. You mustn't make so
many assumptions. They tend to get you in
trouble. Perhaps I'm not free to go. But that
doesn't mean what you might think.

                    PRISONER
Huh?

                     VOICE
          (off)
Let's just drop it… Against the rules.

                    PRISONER
But—

                     VOICE
          (off)
I said drop it.

                    PRISONER
Fine.
          (A non-committal shrug.)
So however it is, you're on their side -
you're helping them?

                    VOICE
     (off)
     (After a moment.)
Whose side?

                  PRISONER
Theirs, you know - those who bested me?

                    VOICE
     (off)
You think somebody bested you?

                  PRISONER
Kinda obvious, I'm here aren't I?
     (resigned)

                    VOICE
     (off)
First of all, any besting that was done, was
done by and to yourself. Wasn't their fault.
And secondly, it certainly wasn't my fault. In
point of fact, my role is inconsequential,
though I do admit that things might have
resulted differently if I'd been better, which
may be what landed me here. Penance of sorts I
suppose.
     (The tone has changed. No longer as
     sardonic; maybe even sincere.)
But on this topic, or a related one, what
makes you right, and special?

                  PRISONER
I'm not special.
     (resigned)

                    VOICE
     (off)
That's not what you said, you said **destiny**.
     (Pounding out the word.)

                  PRISONER
It's not me that's special, it's what I stand
for. *The Solution*.

                    VOICE
     (off)
Oh, *The Solution*; well never mind then. I
never knew…
     (A brass echo.)

                  PRISONER
     (Walking over to his thin damp mat to sit
     down. His voice is quiet but defiant, not
     broken.)
I know your kind. The scoffers. Those who
stand for nothing, using cynicism as a defense
for stupidity - for valueless lives that will
extinguish themselves in a sputter, not a
blast. A waste of skin, serving masters you do
not know for reasons you do not understand for
rewards you do not value. You sicken me, but
you do not move me.

                  THE VOICE
     (off)
There it is! I knew I'd get a speech.
     (Pounding glee.)

     (Silence. Then a clattering at the refuse
     pile gets louder, and the scratching and
     squealing in the dark becomes frenzied.)

PRISONER
You ridicule me because you do not believe,
but it's you who I'm fighting for as well.

VOICE
     (off)
How do you know? You don't know me.

PRISONER
Because I believe. I believe that whoever you
are - you deserve more than that.
     (He points out the tiny window that had
     been painted black.)
Out there, you won't fare any better than I
did - if you choose to believe in something,
in anything.

VOICE
     (off)
What makes you think I don't?

PRISONER
If you did, you either wouldn't be in here, or
you wouldn't be mocking me.

VOICE
     (off)
So you say.

PRISONER
So I say.

VOICE
     (off)
What if you're wrong?

PRISONER

What do you mean?

VOICE
    (off)
What if I believe in everything that destroyed
you? What if that is my idea of future - and
you are my idea of evil? What if you are my
enemy? What if I have been watching you these
last days, weeks, months, years and laughing?
What is it to you why I am stuck here - if you
want to believe that - and what if I tell you
that you being here is worth everything to me?
    (A pause.)
In that case, would I still be what you are
fighting for? If fighting for me means you are
actually fighting yourself? If my defense
results in your final defeat - even if you get
out of here; even if you win this battle?

PRISONER

I don't follow.
    (confusion)
We all have the right to believe as we wish.

VOICE
    (off)
Even if I believe you should die in here?

PRISONER
    (Standing, crossing to the small toilet
    to relieve himself in the dark. The
    tinkling for an instant replaces the
    small claws rattling the metal against
    the far wall.)
I don't think you mean that.

                         VOICE
          (off)
Are your beliefs strong enough to be wrong?
Because here you are. And you're never going
to get out of here.

                       PRISONER
I do believe.

                         VOICE
          (off)
Are you willing to risk everything for that
belief?

                       PRISONER
Well, here I am - sitting here in the dark
with *you*. Isn't that proof enough?

                         VOICE
          (off)
Touché. But I bet you didn't think you'd be
here this long, did you?

                       PRISONER
Freedom is not free.

                         VOICE
          (off)
Don't read me a bumper sticker.

                       PRISONER
These things take time.

                    VOICE
          (off)
Wait, wait. I need a pen to write this stuff
down.

                  PRISONER
The fight against this kind of darkness is not
easy. We are facing all the power that evil
can throw at us. A criminal state. The total
control of our minds, our futures.
Discrimination and violence. Theft. Slavery.
Torture and abuse. And yet still we resist.

                    VOICE
          (off)
Excuses.
          (disgust)
You use excuses to mask your continued failure
and scapegoats to hide your inability to win.

                  PRISONER
I made my case. Here I am, aren't I? Doesn't
that mean I'm a threat to them?

                    VOICE
          (off)
Does it?

                  PRISONER
Being here is a moral victory.

                    VOICE
          (off)
Is it?

PRISONER
My words were true, and *they* could not allow
them to be heard.

VOICE
    (off)
Were they?

PRISONER
Well, they must have been if the state felt it
had to silence me?

VOICE
    (off)
Did it?

PRISONER
My ideas were better. My plan greater. I was
making headway.
    (The prisoner turns to wash his hands in
    the small sink.)

VOICE
    (off)
What ideas? Let me ask you, since you brought
it up. What was new in your message? What were
you selling the people that they have not
already heard or had?
    (bitterness, scorn)

PRISONER
Well, for starters they are so poor—

                    VOICE
          (off)
That's a nice condescension, coming from a
rich man.

                  PRISONER
          (The prisoner turns from his sink to lean
          back against the far wall. The room is
          still dark, though it is well into
          daytime. The white cracks of light have
          grown brighter and thrown a silvery aura
          into the murky room.)
I mean, what I'm trying to say is that people
are *still* poor. Their lives have not been
improved.

                    VOICE
          (off)
Ya, they've been poor forever and they will be
poor forever. Cry me a river. Why does that
give you the right to rule?

                  PRISONER
Not rule, but try and improve their situation.
Help them get out of poverty.

                    VOICE
          (off)
How humanitarian.

                  PRISONER
Somebody has to help them.

                    VOICE
          (off)
Isn't that what the Elders say?

                    PRISONER
Yes, but they are wrong.

                     VOICE
          (off)
Why?

                    PRISONER
Because people are still poor. And the Elders
are so very rich.

                     VOICE
          (off)
So are you. Or at least you were.

                    PRISONER
That's different.

                     VOICE
          (off)
Why?

                    PRISONER
Because, because well… The Elders use food as
a weapon, money as a lever, control as their
end goal. That's it, it's not about the people
but about the Elders' power. I intended to
help the people, to set them free, to empower
them to make their own money and control their
own lives.

                    VOICE
          (off)
Assuming that were true, which I doubt, you
think poverty, and by the same token wealth,
are conditions imposed on people from the
outside? Only waiting for the right recipe?
That poor people are sitting around waiting
for you, so they can become rich?

                  PRISONER
People are stuck.

                    VOICE
          (off)
How did they get stuck, ever wonder about
that?

                  PRISONER
Because they didn't have opportunity. Because
of bad projects by the state. Bad
implementation really, because the motivations
were bad – about power, not about helping the
poor. The collectivities—

                    VOICE
          (off)

          (interrupting)
The collectivities indeed. A bunch of
sniveling opportunists looking for a handout.
You talk about opportunity. But opportunity to
what, if they are just sitting around waiting
for you? You don't think the people that can,
make their own opportunity, and people who
can't maybe just join collectivities?

                    PRISONER
Nobody is an island.

                    VOICE
          (off)
Ah, right, it takes a village. You didn't
build that. You didn't get there on your own.
Now is not the time for profit. Etcetera. Got
it.

                    PRISONER
People need each other to succeed.

                    VOICE
          (off)
People need themselves to succeed.

                    PRISONER
Alone nobody can do anything.

                    VOICE
          (off)
Alone an architect can have a house, a farmer
can eat, and a writer can build a world.
Nobody can farm in community, build
communally, or write collectively. The
division of labor, which you pretend to refer
to, still requires labor.

                    PRISONER
I could have gotten them to work together, I
know it. The rich would have given more, the
poor would have worked harder; through
collaboration and sharing we could achieve
harmony.

                    VOICE
          (off)
Are you going to burst into song?

                  PRISONER
          (Turning his back.)
You can mock, but you would have seen.

                    VOICE
          (off)
I truly wish I could have voted for you, to
see. Oh ya, you decided voting wasn't really
for you.

                  PRISONER
          (Looking over his shoulder.)
That's not true, I gave it a chance, it didn't
work.

                    VOICE
          (off)
You didn't win?

                  PRISONER
Well, no.

                    VOICE
          (off)
Isn't that the whole point of voting?

                  PRISONER
          (Jumping back around to face the voice.)
They system is rigged, I can prove it—

                    VOICE
      (off)
More excuses. But getting to the real
question, what would you do differently, you
and your collectivities? What are you offering
the people besides a different group of pigs
at the trough?

                  PRISONER
Oh, there are so many things we could do.
Building citizenship through shared
opportunity. Grand projects, great public
works that would create jobs.

                    VOICE
      (off)
Like what, name some.

                  PRISONER
Well, for example the road between The Capital
and the regions has pot holes; we could fill
those in and put people to work. In the
forbidden zone there are rumored to be lots of
animals, we could do tourism projects to build
a hotel managed by a cooperative and let
people see their own country. So many people
want to become involved, we could re-organize
the founder's collectives into local councils
and we could allot them money from the budget
to implement their own community projects. We
could let farmers decide what to plant and
then distribute to them seeds and tools - of
course correcting for overplanting one crop. I
would set in place a new ministry of
employment to coordinate the scarce jobs and
help people find work. Kids would be given

back to their parents. Poor children could get scholarships, to study in areas that would increase national productivity. We need welfare programs for the street children. We need subsidies for gasoline so people can get to work, for food and for primary education. We need free health care. We need economic zones and tourist zones and technology zones. We need to subsidize the arts and music to nourish our humanity; and create great programs where we can volunteer of ourselves and our time. All these things could help.

                    VOICE
          (off)
Hmm. All that sounds vaguely familiar. And what do you get out of this?

                    PRISONER
What do you mean?

                    VOICE
          (off)
You heard me. What's in it for you? You've already got - well had - money, position, prestige. Girls, booze. What's in it for you?

                    PRISONER
Well, when you put it that way—

                    VOICE
          (off)
What other way should I put it? You get to rule.

                    PRISONER
Hey—

                     VOICE
          (off)

          (Cutting him off again.)
Never mind, back to the topic at hand. You
named a series of projects.

                    PRISONER
Yes.

                     VOICE
          (off)
I hate to be the guy to have to tell you this,
but they've all been done. Countless times
before, in countless places. And let me share
with you a little secret - we still have poor
people.

                    PRISONER
They weren't done right.
          (defensive)

                     VOICE
          (off)
Something wasn't done right, for sure. What
should make them believe in you?

                    PRISONER
What's that?

                    VOICE
          (off)
Well, the things you're promising. Folks are
getting variations of those same things right
now. A bird in the hand, right? Why should
they, oh let's call it *change the horse in
midstream*.
          (chuckling)

                  PRISONER
Because the Perfect Order is not working.

                    VOICE
          (off)
Sure as shit ain't working for you.

                  PRISONER
          (indignant)
Hey!

                    VOICE
          (off)
Sorry. But seriously, what makes you think you
could have made it work? Better men than you
have tried - and failed.

                  PRISONER
I'm sure we could have found the right
formula.

                    VOICE
          (off)
I'm pretty sure we've all heard that before
too, haven't we?

                    PRISONER
But this time—

                     VOICE
This time? That's what I heard last time, and
the time before, and the time before that.

                    PRISONER
Well what do you propose?

                     VOICE
     (off)
I don't propose. I guess that's why you're
sitting on a urine soaked mattress and I'm
not.
     (a maniacal chuckle)

                    PRISONER
Where are you, anyway?

                     VOICE
     (off)
Don't change the subject. You still never
answered my first question. What's in it for
you?

                    PRISONER
Nothing's in it for me. And I resent you
implying otherwise. I do this because of what
I believe in, for our project and for *The
Solution*. Mine is the greatest sacrifice of
all, the disinterested one.

                    VOICE
          (off)
If I believed you, that would make you the
stupidest man in the world.

                  PRISONER
That's a hell of a thing to say to me.

                    VOICE
          (off)
Is it? Ever watched somebody do something they
didn't find interesting? Its uninspiring at
best, at worst is downright sad. Yet you —
you're willing to sleep in your own urine for
something you don't even find interesting?
That's either insanity or profound stupidity.

                  PRISONER
That's not what disinterested means.

                    VOICE
          (off)
Educate me. What does it mean then?

                  PRISONER
It means that I have no skin in the game, no
horse in the race, no dog in the fight. I do
this only for my love of my fellow men and my
commitment to my ideals.

                    VOICE
          (off)
So something which does not affect your life
at all.

                    PRISONER
Right!

                    VOICE
     (off)
Let me ask you something.

                    PRISONER
Yes?

                    VOICE
     (off)
Would you live in a house that was built by an
architect who did not like his job, did not
require your approval over the designs, did
not need your satisfaction to obtain payment,
and didn't require your recommendation to get
future work? Who had no stake whatsoever in
the house he built for you?

                    PRISONER
Of course not.

                    VOICE
     (off)
Then you should never be allowed to rule.

                    PRISONER
It's different.

                    VOICE
     (off)
How?

PRISONER

Because I do want the job. Me being here, as you well put it, is proof of that. But not for any personal gain.

VOICE

(off)

Right – so it has nothing to do with rewarding your own. Or having people call you *sir*. Seeing your face on TV? Visits to foreign lands; respect? People chanting your name. 'Oh thank you, Mr. Prisoner, sir, for delivering us from *them*'. Seems awfully altruistic. Or is it about the money? Sure, you say you have money – but not *their* kind of money. Not that kind of stolen money which requires no accounting, unlimited in fact. And power, their kind of arbitrary power to do whatever they want, whenever they want with no consequences; especially to people you hate. And, isn't it really more about that?

PRISONER

About what?

VOICE

(off)

Hate. You hate them. They look different, they smell and they talk funny. They like different music, eat different food. They mess things up. They're loud. They'd rather drink beer than whisky. They'd rather bowl than golf. They'd rather talk about sports than theater; they read novelettes and watch movies with scantily clad women. They are uncomfortable;

and they are in charge. And they've done this
to **you**.
        (emphasis on the 'you')
Sure, it's fine if they are the objects of all
your pet projects - your worker training
programs and your pothole-filling experiments.
But *you* calling *them* 'sir'? *You* suffering
under *them*, who are so much less? That's what
The Happening did to your kind, to your people
- who used to rule. And you don't like that
one little bit, do you?

                    PRISONER
        (quietly)
You have no right.

                    VOICE
        (off)
Don't I?

                    PRISONER
No. Absolutely not. How *dare* you question my
motives?

                    VOICE
        (off)
How dare I?

                    PRISONER
Yes, how dare you.

                    VOICE
        (off)
OK, let me tell you how I dare. The second you
sought out political position - the minute you
asked your fellow men for their support, you

opened yourself up to the criticism of every
Tom, Dick and dumbass. You, who so desperately
wanted to be called sir, by asking for their
support invited them to act as amateur judges
on your character, on your qualifications, on
your family life and – yes – on your
motivations. You opened your life up to the
idiots; and this is the result.

                    PRISONER
A people must know their leader.

                     VOICE
          (off)
Ah, yes – the great leader. Because of course
then it got worse – when you couldn't convince
people that your projects were any better than
the ones they already had; and when you
finally pitted your hate against their hate
and you lost, you did the last thing that came
to your mind. You tried to take it. Not with
guns, you don't have any. Not with money, you
haven't stolen enough to hand out. But with a
revolt. Huge piles of dead bodies, that will
get the people's attention! As long as it's
not your body, of course. Isn't that what
September Seventh was about?

                    PRISONER
We did not want the blood. If there were to be
bodies, as there were, they would be people
they killed. To show their true colors.

                         VOICE
          (off)
Not all of 'em.

                       PRISONER
No, not all of them.
          (The prisoner walks again to the window,
saddened by a thought or a memory.)
But that wasn't my fault.
          (Without conviction.)

                         VOICE
          (off)
But aren't you the great leader? Never mind,
rhetorical question. You can't tell me that
you weren't preparing to get your rag-tag army
slaughtered.

                       PRISONER
We all participated willingly.

                         VOICE
          (off)
Sure, they thought maybe you were gonna win –
and could hand out privileges denied by *them*.
Besides, your people don't like *them* much
either, do they? And for the same reasons you
don't. But the dead? They were expendable, you
were not. They were leaderless, you were the
leader. And you were pretty too, which helps.
The tools you use to rule – their blood for
your power.

PRISONER

No

    (He is again defiant, shaking his fist in
    the air.)

It was not about the blood or the power - it
was about the right to be free. The dream of
living an uncoerced life, of walking alone,
guided by your own conscience. To not have to
surrender to the arbitrary will of an overlord
but keep the quiet privacy of our own company
in our own community. This is what the people
clamor for. This is what the people want.
Freedom.

VOICE

    (off)

Freedom. OK, I have a deal. We'll put freedom
in my left hand, a ham sandwich in my right
and go out into the slums. Let's see which
hand people pick. Besides, what happened to
your talk about poor people? I don't see them
using the word 'freedom' very much. Hard to be
free when you're hungry. Or was it freedom for
you and the soup kitchen for them?

PRISONER

That's not fair.

                    VOICE
          (off)
Why not? Appears to me that what you are
offering is less of the good stuff and more of
something that can't be washed down with a
beer. Say, by the way. Freedom. Do I eat that
with a fork or with a spoon? It isn't too
spicy, is it? I've got irritable bowel
syndrome.
          (more cackling laughter)

                  PRISONER
          (Ignores the comment.)
The greatest struggle in human existence is
the struggle to be free. People surrender
their fortunes, their livelihoods, their loved
ones and even their lives for this vision.

                    VOICE
          (off)
People. Which people?

                  PRISONER
People who know that to say what they believe
is worth any cost.

                    VOICE
          (off)
Ever ridden the subway?

                  PRISONER
Of course, is that another rich jab?

<pre>
                    VOICE
          (off)
Maybe, but my point is have you ever listened
to the conversations of 'the people' on the
subway?

                  PRISONER
Sometimes.

                    VOICE
          (off)
Freedom to say what they want? To express
what's in their hearts? Their greatest
yearnings? People talk about the women they
bedded. Their hangover from Saturday night.
Their opinion of the latest slasher movie. Who
won the lottery. Nobody is talking about the
state, or the Elders - tyranny and liberty;
only you kids do that. Everybody else is
wrapped up in their small lives. I'm not sure
people should be allowed to die for the right
to that rubbish.

                  PRISONER
People yearn to be free - that is what
revolutions are made from.

                    VOICE
          (off)
Again I ask you, who are these people, per
chance?

                  PRISONER
Ordinary people, just like you and me.
</pre>

VOICE
(off)
First, you are not ordinary. I know your
pedigree. Second, how do you know I am?

PRISONER
(A quiet pattering starts to hit against
the window pane. Rain. The Prisoner
cranes his neck to catch a sight,
twisting his nose for the telltale scent
of mustiness that accompanies a storm.
But the small window only gives the
slightest hint of a world outside.
Nevertheless he reaches up to wipe around
the small window, hoping for some touch
of the moisture and finding it, spreads
it on his cheeks.)
The popular clamor is undeniable, even if you
can't see it. The State knows that and that's
why it fears me; which is why I'm here.

VOICE
(off)
Oh, wait. I think I hear them now.
(The voice rises in mock alarm.)
They are marching. 'Can you hear the people
sing, singing the songs of angry men'. They
are raising barricades. The system is falling.
It's crumbling before our eyes. The music of
triumph, of revolt. The winds of change! Oh,
my bad, that's just the factory workers headed
out to a topless bar at the end of their
shift.

PRISONER
They will come—

                    VOICE
          (off)
The cause of freedom. Your great cause. I hate
to break it to you. However it appears you
have been forgotten. How long have you been
here now?

                  PRISONER
I can't remember.

                    VOICE
          (off)
Yes you can - but if you admit it to me,
you'll have to admit it to yourself. That you
were abandoned. You were left alone. Nobody is
coming.

                  PRISONER
          (Whispered denial.)
That is not true. It can't be. We all agreed
they would come. We made plans. The Solution
required a martyr.

                    VOICE
          (off)
The Solution required an idiot, a temper
tantrum of adolescent impertinence. But yes,
you were needed, but not by your 'Solution'.
It is *they* who required you - but not as a
martyr, as an example.

                  PRISONER
Nelson Mandela once said—

                         VOICE
        (off)
Argh, not again! Nelson Mandela. I'm so sick
of him. Every Phil, Fred and jackass think
they are the reincarnation of good old Nelson.
You know, Nelson wasn't all that great either.
He required a whole lot of work. Had to take a
long vacation after that one.
        (mumbling)

                       PRISONER
What? You knew Mandela?

                         VOICE
        (off)
Oh, ya in passing, but that doesn't matter.

                       PRISONER
What was he like?

                         VOICE
        (off)
He didn't spend his time asking what you are
like, if you want the truth. Nelson has made
my job so much harder; I don't want to talk
about it. It does bring a question to mind for
you, however. How many people were imprisoned
with good old Nelson; or in any countless
number of other countries over history? Tens,
thousands, millions? Who are they? What are
their names? How were they arrested? What did
they fight for? What happened to their
families? What were their grand *solutions*?"

                    PRISONER
Well, I ah…

                     VOICE
          (off)

          (interrupting)
Where are their names written? Is there a
pristine martyr's beach in the great beyond
where they have met up to share stories? Do
they get a special pass to heaven? Is there an
express lane? Do they get lap dances from the
angels, does Saint Peter buy them a beer?

                    PRISONER
I don't know.

                     VOICE
          (off)
You don't know.
          (mocking)
Could that be because nobody knows? Because
for every great man who frees his people –
supposing they were actually enslaved in the
first place, or supposing they wanted to be
free in any event – how many do you think
perished? How many were unheard of? How many
lost their families, their livelihoods, their
lives? You have no idea.

                    PRISONER
          (The painful silence is broken only
          broken by the sounds of a choking,
          sputtering sob.)
This… is… my… destiny…

                         VOICE
          (off)
So you keep saying. I don't think that word
means what you think it means. You use it
mostly as a defense against your panic. So too
have others. Pushing fate, forcing destiny's
hand. Bold, dangerous. Arrogant. Stupid.

                       PRISONER
You will see. If nothing is sacrificed,
nothing can ever be won. I am happy to
sacrifice myself on the altar of freedom. The
ideas we strive for are worth the fight,
though they require our greatest sacrifice.

                         VOICE
          (off)
Right, the ideas of freedom. More worker
training programs, food baskets that do not
require a party card, public service jobs that
do not demand marching and saluting. Way to
think big!

                       PRISONER
What would you suggest then?

                         VOICE
          (off)
I told you once, I don't suggest.

                       PRISONER
Then what gives you the right to criticize?
Who are you anyway? You seem to be sent here
only to torment me.

                    VOICE
          (off)
If you must know, I am. I attend to the dreams
of the defeated; and when I must I get
involved. You may not see me; no, better put,
you cannot see me. Don't bother to keep
asking, you'll never figure it out. Besides,
it doesn't matter anyway. Who I am won't help
you - and you're at the moment of your
greatest need.

                  PRISONER
What does that mean?

                    VOICE
          (off)
You are about to become lost forever - and I
have no time to help the forever-lost.

                  PRISONER
How's that? You want to… Help me? Like, help
me get out of here?

                    VOICE
          (off)
I didn't say that. But let's say I did. Would
you accept it? Even if it came in a form you
did not recognize?

                  PRISONER
Er, well, I don't know. I suppose I'd have to
know who you are.

                    VOICE
          (off)
Boy you are persistent. Who, like I told you
before, does not matter. It's what that
matters. There have been many who warmed the
spaces behind the rusted bars in the dungeon
prisons of this world. Those who were saved
were not saved by answering who - but by
answering what, and why. The key to their
freedom was not on which side they happened to
be, but by what they came to believe about
their captivity - or more specifically the
nature of captivity in the first place. Even
your precious Nelson, although it took him
almost thirty years to learn. Besides, as
things are going you're never going to get out
of here anyway, so no point speculating.

                  PRISONER
OK, fine. If for no other reason than boredom,
I'll hear you out.
          (haughty)

                    VOICE
          (off)
That's not gonna work for me. I've got a lot
of other people to see who are not as much
work as you. To tell you the truth, I'm a
little tired and not up to the task right now.
I've been doing this for a long time - each
time I think I'm making progress I look up and
find I'm further behind. It's exhausting.

                  PRISONER
What's exhausting?

                    VOICE
          (off)
You are, right now.

                    PRISONER
You can leave.

                    VOICE
          (off)
Can I?

                    PRISONER
Can't you?

                    VOICE
          (off)
Maybe, but then what would you do?

                    PRISONER
What do you mean?

                    VOICE
          (off)
Well, how do I put this? Your escape plan
seems to be flawed. Nobody is coming. Do you
have a plan B?

                    PRISONER
     Not exactly.

                    VOICE
          (off)
So what are you going to do? Your trial is
coming up, is it not?

PRISONER

Yes, it is. Although they keep scheduling it
and putting it off. I've been waiting so long,
I've forgotten how long. Besides the waiting,
I don't know; I suppose hanging on for
destiny. Or for providence. For the other shoe
to drop. You know, sometimes you put your head
down and just wait; cuz something's gotta
give.

VOICE

(off)

Great strategy. Well anyway that gives us some
time; time to plan your defense, not that it's
gonna matter.

PRISONER

It wasn't supposed to be like this. This was
not the plan.

VOICE

(off)

It never is. But such as it is, consider our
encounter as the destiny you so want to
believe in, if it helps.

PRISONER

That does help.

VOICE

(off)

All right, let's get down to it.

(CURTAIN)

(END OF ACT)

ACT II

Scene 1

SETTING: A courtroom. On the left the judge sits behind the bench, two feet above the witness stand. Beside the judge is a flag flying the national colors; purple, orange and green. The symbol on the flag is a CCTV camera below the words: "Security, Truth, and Fear". Facing the audience to the left of the bench is the defendant's dais. Up above the judge and to the right is a screen where a video can be projected. To the right of the bench and below the screen, facing the judge's bench is the witness stand, opposite the defendant's box. The audience serves as the observers to the trial.

AT RISE: The prisoner stands, defiant, in the defendant's box. His hands are in front of him, handcuffed, and rested on the edge of the box. He has aged from scene one. His countenance is no longer that of a young man, but of a prisoner worn down by the lack of sunlight and nutritious food, but more by the absence of hope. His hair has grayed and is long and knotted; there are cuts and bruises on his face, which has been shaved. He is dressed in a cheap wrinkled suit, patched and re-sewn with a tie that does not match. The judge is an elegant woman, dressed in a flowing robe, upon her head is a red velvet hat. She has makeup applied liberally, her hair is specially arranged and died. Her fingernails are stick-on and colorful.

According to the law, there were no lawyers or juries, only accuser, accused and judge.

JUDGE
    (Clearing her throat and pounding her
    gavel.)
Today we hear the case of the people against Prisoner #28957. The prisoner is charged with rebellion, conspiracy and destruction of property, and murder.
    (A murmur ripples through the audience,
    who cannot be seen.)
But worst of all, the prisoner is charged with the most heinous thought crimes imaginable. Betrayal of our party values, challenging the morality of our dear leaders, rejecting the *Perfect Order* and conspiracy to deny the deity of the founder. If found guilty, any one of these crimes is punishable by death but together they comprise the most nefarious acts ever contemplated against the party and the state. If found guilty, the prisoner will be publicly tortured for seven days and then executed, with his body cut into pieces and sent to the regions as a lesson to those who imagine there to be another way. We now call on the defendant to face his accusers. Then the people's court will decide the fate of those who refuse to obey the law and submit.

ACCUSER
(Walks from the right to step up on the
small dais. The accuser has her head
covered by a blue cloth bag. Her voice is
harmonious, its sing-song chirp out of
place in the austere environment of the
court.)
Your honor, as per my right according to the
law, I am choosing to withhold my identity
from the court and the defendant.
(A deep breath.)
I stand ready to accuse the prisoner of
rebellion.
(Turning her head to the prisoner.)

JUDGE
(Turning her gaze from accuser to
prisoner)
Prisoner, how do you plead?

PRISONER
I plead not guilty.
(Murmurs through the court. The prisoner
is sober. He is quiet and subdued and
serious; without the violent hope of his
prison days. Not defeated, but not unruly
anymore either.)
But not for the reasons that you think.

JUDGE
Nevertheless, you have pled not guilty. The
accuser will endeavor to demonstrate to the
court that you are, in fact, guilty.

ACCUSER
Thank you your honor.
      (The accuser turns to face the prisoner.)
Do you remember where you were on September
seventh?

PRISONER
      (Shaking his head.)
There have been a great many September
sevenths in my lifetime.

ACCUSER
You know what I'm referring to.

PRISONER
Yes, I know what you're referring to.

ACCUSER
Where were you then?

PRISONER
The place is called the meadows; but I'm sure
you know that.

JUDGE
Restrict your answers to the questions asked
please.

ACCUSER
Tell us about it.

                    PRISONER
         (As the prisoner narrates, a video
         showing the meadows is projected on the
         screen above.)
Not far outside the iron gates of the city,
beyond the two barbed wire walls with the mine
field in between them and over the moat; past
the barking of the Dobermans and the clanking
of the boots on the walls that ring the
capital and down the main motor way, avoiding
the craters left by the scatter bombs, you
will find a narrow dirt road going west.
         (The courtroom was silent.)

                    ACCUSER
Go on.
         (Almost kind.)

                    PRISONER
         (Taking a deep breath.)
This road goes for several miles through the
forest. The pine trees hug the road; they
smell so fresh after the stench of pollution
and smog in the capital. It's been so long
since I've smelled trees—

                    JUDGE
I instruct you to answer the question.

                    PRISONER
         (Smiling, a peaceful memory.)
You can't even see the statue of the founder
from there. I'd never been anywhere where you
couldn't see his statue.

                    JUDGE
I order you to get to the point.

                  PRISONER
          (Turning to look at the judge.)
That is what I'm doing your honor. Down that
way a while you can find an old building - I
think it must have been a church once, but
since I'd never seen one that's only a guess.
          (Gasps from the audience.)
I was alone, it felt so good to be alone.
Privacy. To stand naked and unafraid.

                   ACCUSER
You admit you were illegally nude; without
even The Order's perfect coverings?

                  PRISONER
It's a turn of phrase. Rhetorical flourish if
you will.

                    JUDGE
Stick to the facts.

                  PRISONER
Yes your honor.

                   ACCUSER
          (Stepping down from the witness stand to
          pace between the prisoner and the judge.)
How did you obtain the pass to leave the
capitol?

                  PRISONER
I was on a student exchange.

                    ACCUSER
Aren't those programs reserved for the state's
best students?

                    PRISONER
Yes, I was a son of a party family, and
groomed as one of the brightest minds.

                    ACCUSER
        (Stopping pacing, to turn toward the
        prisoner.)
So you obtained special privileges?

                    PRISONER
Privileges you may consider them, but they are
not the state's to mete out.

                    JUDGE
Be careful, prisoner, or you will be found in
contempt. Did you or did you not have special
privileges?

                    PRISONER
Yes, according to you.

                    ACCUSER
        (Walking back in the direction of her
        stand.)
What made you take the gifts that the state
generously gave you and use them for the
purposes of betrayal?
        (The accuser lashes out wickedly, then
        says more slowly.)
Never mind, we'll get to that. Tell us about
the meadows.

                    PRISONER
This old church, I found it when I was biking
back from my Founder's Fellowship. You see, I
had been assigned propaganda activities in one
of the quadrants. I saw the little road and
decided to take it. I had made good time - I
was in better condition than most - and didn't
have to punch my physical presence card for
several more hours. The little church has no
traces of *the violence* at all - it's just
abandoned and old, not destroyed. It sits in a
beautiful open meadow with dandelions and
thick, soft green grass. That's why we call it
the meadows.

                    ACCUSER
By the way, who is we?

                    PRISONER
        (quickly)
I mean I.

                    ACCUSER
Who is we?

                    PRISONER
There is no we, I was just thinking about a
little dog that I had found in the church.

                    ACCUSER
You are of course lying. But go on. What
happened on September seventh?

PRISONER

I went into the little church. It was lovely,
the old wooden benches and the pulpit at the
front. The stained glass was all beaten out
and small animals were living in the rafters
but it smelled clean and wholesome.

ACCUSER

What did you find there?

PRISONER

I found peace.

ACCUSER

No, I mean what thing did you find there?

PRISONER

I found a ream of paper.
      (Gasps from the audience.)

ACCUSER

An unregistered ream of paper?

PRISONER

Yes.

ACCUSER

And what did you do with it?

PRISONER

At first nothing. I kept it safe, hidden in
the church.

ACCUSER

But you returned.

PRISONER
Yes.

ACCUSER
And did you take anything with you that time?

PRISONER
My sense of wonder.
     (Smiling tiredly)

JUDGE
     (Leaning forward with her finger
     outstretched.)
One more answer like that and you will be
found in contempt.

PRISONER
Yes ma'am.

ACCUSER
What did you take with you?

PRISONER
A pencil.
     (gasps)

ACCUSER
A pencil. Where did you get a pencil from?

PRISONER
I took it from my university.

ACCUSER
And what did you tell the minders had happened
to it?

PRISONER

I told them it had fallen through the storm
drain when I had slipped on the marble walkway
in front of the Hall of Elders, which was wet
from the rain.

ACCUSER

        (Stepping onto the witness stand again.)
You lied, and you misappropriated the goods of
the state. That is bad enough. But what did
you do with the pencil?

PRISONER

At night I would exercise to improve my
stamina, to make me faster. Everywhere I ran.
On my ration recuperation days I ran to and
from the centers furthest from my house. Every
two days during prayer hour I would run to the
temples farthest away to light the candle and
make the prayers of fear and gratitude to the
founder. I ran everywhere; people called me a
fool and not a few minders began taking note.
I became hard and fast. All this so that
whenever I was sent away on the Founders
Fellowship work I was able to peel away
several hours - the estimated travel times are
set for weak men, and fat. I would go to the
little church, and I would write.

ACCUSER

Writing. Unsanctioned writing on unregistered
paper with a stolen pencil.

PRISONER

        (Defiant but resigned.)
If you say so.

ACCUSER
What happened on September seventh?

PRISONER
September seventh was one of the times I went
to the meadows.

ACCUSER
What was different about this time?

PRISONER
I think it might have been raining.

ACCUSER
Don't lie to the court. What was different
about this time?
     (silence)
I will tell you, since you refuse. That day
you took somebody else with you.
     (The courtroom bursts into a cacophony.)

JUDGE
     (Hitting her gavel on the bench.)
Order. I demand order in the court.

ACCUSER
Who was it?

PRISONER
I don't know what you're talking about.

JUDGE
Lying to the court is punishable by ten years
in solitary confinement. Who was it?

PRISONER
(Only looks up at the video above the
judge.)

ACCUSER
I would like to submit into evidence this
satellite photograph, date stamped September
seventh, clearly showing two people entering
the building in the open meadow outside the
capitol.
(Another round of commotion.)
Who was it? Who was it?
(The accuser screams, shrill in the
closed air of the court.)
Who was it!?

PRISONER
I thought alone, I wrote alone, I acted alone.
I alone am responsible for September seventh.
That's all you will get from me.

ACCUSER
(Calmer)
It is of no importance anyway, we already
know.
(The prisoner shows no emotion.)
Why did you take somebody else to the meadows?
(The prisoner refuses to answer.)

JUDGE
Answer, so that the court may be lenient with
you.

PRISONER
(The prisoner appears conflicted for a
moment, then a look of resignation
appears across his worn face.)
I wanted them to experience the sensation of
being alone. Of self-isolation. Of freedom.

JUDGE
Do not use that word. You know very well that
word has been stricken from the official
lexicon. See you do not repeat the offense.

PRISONER
Yes your honor.

ACCUSER
Why did you want them to experience…
(Searching for a word.)
Solitude? Do you hate your fellow man?

PRISONER
Hate is an emotion I no longer have the energy
for.

ACCUSER
But you did hate the state?

PRISONER
For a time, I hated those who saw themselves
as my betters. Who believed they had the right
to dictate my behavior, my food and
entertainment, my thoughts.

ACCUSER
It has been scientifically proven that
individual thoughts are flawed. Only thoughts
preserved by the collective through the state
have any value - why would you want to waste
your time with useless, inefficient, imperfect
thoughts? What good is that for humanity?

PRISONER
Who said I wanted to do anything good for
humanity?

ACCUSER
     (baffled)
What else are you alive for?

PRISONER
I once thought like you, even while I secretly
opposed you. Now I realize I was wrong. I am
the reason for my own existence.

ACCUSER
That makes no sense. It has been proven that
only in service to your fellow man is your
life worth anything. Your thoughts are arcane,
undisciplined, inferior.

PRISONER
     (smiling)
Then what are you worried about? Why are you
scared of me?

JUDGE
We are asking the questions here.

                    ACCUSER
         (Moving on quickly.)
So you wanted your friend to experience
solitude.

                    PRISONER
I wanted them to know what it was like to
stand alone, without anybody watching.

                    ACCUSER
         (Waving the satellite photo.)
There is never nobody watching.
         (The prisoner shrugged.)
Then what did you do?

                    PRISONER
We began talking.

                    ACCUSER
What were you talking about?

                    PRISONER
The conversation started as we sat watching
the rolling of the grass and the worms
churning through the rich dark earth. Did you
know there are still places not affected by
the radiation? Where the green flourishes?

                    JUDGE
Prisoner.

                    PRISONER
Yes your honor?

JUDGE
You will be careful with your responses. Your
fate depends on it.

ACCUSER
Then what happened?

PRISONER
We talked for as long as we could. When the
time came to go, we agreed to meet again the
next time we had propaganda work to do.

ACCUSER
And did you meet again?

PRISONER
Yes, we met again. But this time—

ACCUSER
This time you were more.

PRISONER
Yes.

ACCUSER
And what did you talk about with them?

PRISONER
We talked about what people are always talking
about, when you people cannot listen.

JUDGE
And what, per se, is that?

PRISONER
We talked about… Well, about something I'm evidently not allowed to mention here.

ACCUSER
Then what happened?

PRISONER
Then, everything changed. Then we had our chance - or so we thought; a new opportunity. Because then your elders called for elections.

JUDGE
      (Looking up from behind her bench to
      scold the prisoner.)
They are your elders too. Prisoner, if you continue down your path of challenge to this court I cannot guarantee your safety.

PRISONER
My safety?

JUDGE
Yes, your physical security.

PRISONER
      (incredulous)
You guarantee *my* physical safety? Your honor, do you know what they have done to me in prison; for you to say you are safeguarding my security? Even I have limits, your honor, limits beyond which even I cannot endure; after such a time as I have had.

                    ACCUSER
          (interrupting)
Let's return to the question. What did you do
then?

                    PRISONER
          (Returning his gaze to the accuser.)
There was an election on, we did what all
loyal subjects did. We started to organize a
platform.

                    ACCUSER
And you called it…?

                    PRISONER
September Seventh.

                    ACCUSER
And your campaign was called?

                    PRISONER
The Solution.

                    ACCUSER
So you admit you formed this organization?

                    PRISONER
          (perking up)
Of course. I am immensely proud of it.

                    ACCUSER
Then why have you pled not guilty?

                    PRISONER
Because what I did was not rebellion. But not
for the reasons you think.

                         ACCUSER
You started a movement. An illegal
organization.

                         PRISONER
Yes.

                         ACCUSER
You know why it was illegal?

                         PRISONER
We were to be allowed only individual
candidates, platforms; but are forbidden
alternative *parties* with governing plans that
diverged from the perfect order.

                         ACCUSER
Your plan was to advance an alternative vision
of the state using an illegal movement?

                         PRISONER
Yes. To a degree.

                         ACCUSER
You sought to devise a plan which would oppose
our all-knowing party and the wisdom of the
elders.
          (The accuser sounds perplexed.)

                         PRISONER
I did that.

                         ACCUSER
Then how were you not engaged in an act of
rebellion?

                    PRISONER
It's quite simple. I was part of your grand
plan.
          (Shuffling of papers fills the room as
          the accuser searches through papers in
          front of her. Over the microphone that
          remained on, the judge's heavy breathing
          can be heard.)

                    ACCUSER
          (looking up)
I don't know what you are referring to.

                    PRISONER
Why was September Seventh started?

                    ACCUSER
I'm asking the questions here.

                    JUDGE
Not so fast. I'll allow it.

                    ACCUSER
Well, er. I suppose… I mean from what I've
heard…
          (more rustling)
According to the manifesto, it was to present
an alternative within the context of the
elections that the elders planned to hold to
allow the nation to demonstrate their love for
the perfect order and their loyalty to the
memory of the founder.

PRISONER
That's right. The elections were called. The
rules for participation were printed in the
gazette. There was even going to be allowed,
at long last, opposing candidates, to a
certain measure. This would allow the state,
through its intimidation and cheating—

JUDGE
Careful. The state does not intimidate, and
neither does it cheat.

PRISONER
    (ironically)
My apologies your honor.

JUDGE
You may go on.

PRISONER
As I was saying, opposing candidates were to
be allowed. We, those of us who believed in
September Seventh, were vying to lead that
option.

ACCUSER
Correct. You were challenging the state.

PRISONER
Not at all.

ACCUSER
You have said it yourself. You were seeking a
different model.

PRISONER

We were actors in a charade established by the elders. Do you really think we had a chance to win in this election?

ACCUSER

    (offended)

You had no chance because there is no opposing the wisdom of the elders and the perfect order of our glorious state.

PRISONER

Who counts the votes?

ACCUSER

Excuse me?

PRISONER

I said, who counts the votes? Who allots airtime for the candidates? Who pays for the propaganda being printed and approves which messages will be allowed? Who organizes the debates? Who chooses the moderators? Who counts the votes? Who counts the votes I ask you?

ACCUSER

    (hysterical)

SHUT UP!

PRISONER

We had no more chance of winning that election than I have leaving here a free man.

ACCUSER
(enraged, foam spews from her mouth)
You will not leave because you are a rabble
rouser. You are guilty of acts of rebellion.

PRISONER
(calmly)
On the contrary, as I have laid out above, the
acts we engaged in were not rebellious at all.
We played within the rules established by the
state and never at any moment were we a threat
to the state. Even worse, we were helping
them. By allowing them a symbol to point at as
they continued to brutalize the people; by
giving their stranglehold on the population
the aura of legitimacy; by lending our names
to a fraud and our labor in the construction
of our own prisons - prisons run by the elders
and from which there is no escape - not only
are we not engaged in acts of rebellion; we
should be given a medal of gratitude from the
state for so enthusiastically participating in
their plan. No, I am not guilty - for the very
reason that you should be grateful; there was
no rebellion, only collusion.
        (The accuser moves from the witness stand
        down toward the prisoner, as if to strike
        him.)

JUDGE
You may step aside.
        (Rage barely contained.)

                    ACCUSER
          (Stopping, from the court floor looking
          up.)
But your honor!

                    JUDGE
          (Standing, waving her fist at the
          accuser.)
You will withdraw!

                    (BLACKOUT)

                    (END OF SCENE)

Scene 2

SETTING: The same court room, the following day. The judge looks more beleaguered. She has no makeup on and three of her nails are missing. She has rings under her eyes, and her hat is off kilter. The Prisoner has been cleaned slightly, a different blue suit, neater and with less tatters, has replaced the other one and his hair is cut.

FADE IN: The prisoner is standing on the box, still handcuffed. The judge is slouching slightly in her chair. The witness stand is empty.

                    JUDGE
          (Pounding her gavel.)
The court is now in session, continuing with the trial of Prisoner #28957. We will now hear from our second witness, party to the charge related to acts of conspiracy and destruction of property, and murder.
          (The witness appears right. He is wearing
          a t-shirt and jeans. He is roughly the
          same age as the prisoner, blond with a
          goatee.)
How do you know the prisoner?

                    WITNESS
          (Looking at the judge, avoiding the
          prisoner.)
We know each other well.
          (The prisoner's face fills with shock.)

JUDGE
Please explain.

WITNESS
We were party to the same crime, your honor. I
was one of the co-founders of September
Seventh. I advanced the mission, assisted in
the planning, and organized the activities. I
was the prisoner's most trusted man.

PRISONER
But why?
     (confused and sad)

WITNESS
     (The witness turned to the prisoner, eyes
     filled with sorrow.)
There is no why, my old friend. There is only
now.
     (sadness)

JUDGE
What do you stand as witness to?

WITNESS
     (Turning back to the judge, all
     business.)
I, well I stand here as a witness and a party
to acts of conspiracy and destruction of
property. And of murder.
     (A flutter went through the court.)

JUDGE
Prisoner, how do you plead?

PRISONER
Again, your honor, I plead not guilty. But,
again, not for the reasons that this witness
will describe.

JUDGE
     (To the witness.)
Were you ever with the prisoner at the
meadows?

WITNESS
Yes, your honor.

JUDGE
How many times?

WITNESS
Countless times.

JUDGE
In your opinion, witness, when did the
prisoner's organization, this September
Seventh, begin its acts of criminal
conspiracy?

WITNESS
That is hard to say, ma'am. Well, there were
many times that… You know, people talk and
it's hard to distinguish idle chatter from
real plotting. What I mean to say is that—

PRISONER
     (interjecting)
It was after the elections.

                    WITNESS
          (Turning to the prisoner, surprised.)
I thought you said you were not guilty?

                    PRISONER
I am not guilty.

                    WITNESS
But you do admit that we began conspiring
after the elections.

                    PRISONER
If that is the way you wish to interpret it.

                    JUDGE
          (To the witness.)
Tell us what happened.

                    WITNESS
It was the night after the elections. The
results had been expected. But the way it was
done—

                    JUDGE
The prisoner did not accept the results?

                    PRISONER
          (Hard, firm with his lips pursed.)
No, I did not.

                    JUDGE
Please explain.

PRISONER
The candidate of September Seventh was not on
the ballot. We had worked hard, made our case
in the limited arenas we were allowed and the
extremely limited minds of men living under
oppression. We had challenged the Platform for
the right to face the elders and their state;
and had bested them. But on Election Day, we
were not even there. Worse, the scanners
rejected our identity marks; anybody who had
sided with September Seventh was not even
allowed to vote.

JUDGE
(shrugging)
Every election has glitches.

PRISONER
(Angry, almost yelling.)
Every single voter from our rosters was
excluded. It was systematic.

JUDGE
The Ministry of Popular Engagement carried out
an investigation and found that it was just
random.

PRISONER
(rage)
Lies. We played by the rules, we registered.
What else did you want?

                    JUDGE
          (carefully)
It was random. Nevertheless, as for the
removal of your 'candidate', your organization
was told multiple times that rejecting the
deity of the founder was grounds for
disqualification. Your organization made a
choice, now you must live with it.

                  PRISONER
We never touched upon the founder.

                    JUDGE
Exactly.

                  PRISONER
So I am being judged for what we did not say?

                    JUDGE
          (Playing with a pen.)
Rebellion is not always overt, sometimes its
most sinister forms come in strategic
ambiguity.

                  PRISONER
I thought I had answered the charge of
rebellion.

                    JUDGE
          (A sly smile.)
True enough. Witness, please proceed.

WITNESS

Prisoner.
>   (Adopting a formal tone, avoiding looking
>   at the prisoner and addressing instead
>   above his head.)

When your election ploy failed to overthrow
the elders, what did you do?

PRISONER

The activities of September Seventh entered a
new phase.

WITNESS

What was this phase?

PRISONER

The phase of active resistance.

WITNESS

And what exactly does this mean?

PRISONER

The plan was simple, as you well know.
>   (The witness does not flinch.)

Attempt to make life miserable for the state.

WITNESS

And what did this plan consist of?

                    PRISONER
         (On the screen above video played of
         riots, of rats running through streets
         and people banging pots.)
Anything that we could think of. We put sugar
in the gas tanks of party members. We released
rats during party congresses. We interrupted
party speeches with the clanging of pans. We
organized to drain the reservoir by us all
leaving the water running during our one hour
time slot. We distributed pamphlets. We held
parties without permits. We wrote songs
without the party censor approving them, we
printed poetry in graffiti on the sides of
walls in blue - a color forbidden since The
Happening. We passed jokes about the elders.
We drew comics about the founder. We had sex
without advising the Secretariat of National
Reproduction.
         (shrugging)
We would not be quiet any longer.

                    WITNESS
But it didn't stop there, did it?

                    PRISONER
Well…

                    WITNESS
Did it??

                    PRISONER
There are some things…

                    WITNESS
DID IT?!

                    JUDGE
You will answer the question.

                  PRISONER
There are some things I can't control.
      (Rage finally bubbling over.)

                   JUDGE
You will hold your anger.

                  PRISONER
Yes your honor.

                  WITNESS
      (Feigning nonchalance.)
What happened, that which was out of your
control?

                  PRISONER
You were there. And it was your fault.

                   JUDGE
The witness is not on trial here.

                  PRISONER
      (To the judge, pointing at the witness
        without looking at him.)
That's because he sold us out. He turned to
you to get out of what happened.

                   JUDGE
ENOUGH.
      (The judge was suddenly angry.)

                    WITNESS
          (Quiet, distantly.)
What did happen?

                    PRISONER
There was a small group, a movement within the
movement if you will, which thought that we
were not going far enough. Motivated by hate,
they sought a more direct reckoning.

                    WITNESS
What was this movement called?

                    PRISONER
It was still September Seventh.

                    WITNESS
An organization that you continued to lead?

                    PRISONER
Yes.

                    WITNESS
Go on.

                    PRISONER
They believed that the small nuisances we were
creating would never be enough to dislodge the
state. The elders and their party were too
strong; despite all the hunger, the misery,
the death. They seemed to think that the
system needed not pinpricks but a massive
shove.

                    WITNESS
Did you think they were right?

PRISONER

I never told them that they were wrong. I
believed it was too risky; and I believed that
if we caused more generalized mayhem the
elders and the state would crack down on
everybody - and people would turn on September
Seventh. We were just starting to gain
credibility.

WITNESS

Did you think they were wrong?

PRISONER

No, I did not. I believed that there would be
a moment when we needed a grand act of
sabotage - of violence. We only differed on
the timing. The moment was not right.

WITNESS

More about the when, not the what?

PRISONER

So I thought. Why are you asking me all this
anyway, why don't you tell them?

JUDGE

May I remind you that the witness is not on
trial here. YOU were the leader of September
Seventh, and YOU are ultimately responsible
for the acts of its members.

PRISONER

Yes, I accept that.

                    JUDGE
Yet you still plead not guilty?

                  PRISONER
I do.

                  WITNESS
Then what happened?

                  PRISONER
The breakaway faction started getting more
brutal. There was first the assault of a
Thought Officer. Then there was the burning
down of one of the houses of a Truth-Teller
from the Ministry of Truth.
     (An extended silence.)

                    JUDGE
What did you do to correct the actions?

                  PRISONER
     (A whisper.)
Nothing.
                    JUDGE
     Speak louder.

                  PRISONER
     (boldly)
I did nothing your honor.

                    JUDGE
Did you speak to them?

PRISONER

No, I was busy. No, that's not true, I was afraid of them. I was worried about my position of leadership. I thought if I confronted them directly then they would break off and we would have divided the movement.
     (Silence, the audience appeared to be
     holding its breath.)

JUDGE

Were you ever planning on dealing with them?
     (The judge had taken over the role of
     questioner after the witness had fallen
     silent.)

PRISONER

Yes, I believed after our big coup, I would have the advantage to take the case to the movement's leadership once and for all. You see, we were arriving to the time of the Founder's Festival - and all the preparations were being set in place. The tents had been set up, the food had been shipped in; special food like meat that we only get once a year. The beer carts were set up; not the normal liquor distilled from antifreeze and cleaning solution; real beer. The event was to last all day.

JUDGE

But it didn't.

PRISONER

No, it didn't.

                    JUDGE
Why not?

                  PRISONER
We had planned something spectacular. There
were to be parallel acts of sabotage. The food
was to cause people to get sick, there was to
be a fireworks display with the colors of the
movement, and the music had been changed from
the anthem of The Happening to that forbidden
since the arrival of the perfect order –
classical music. Finally, we were going to
explode paint bombs under the elders' armored
booths – in blue – just at the time of the
oath of loyalty.

                    JUDGE
But that wasn't all that happened, was it.

                  PRISONER
No.
        (silence)

                    JUDGE
Well?

                   WITNESS
        (Finally looking up from the spot on the
        floor he'd been focusing on, his words
        were anxious – a plea.)
Please, your honor. Not that.

                    JUDGE
What else?

WITNESS

No.
    (He was whimpering.)
He's already admitted his guilt. Can't we move
on?

JUDGE

What happened?

WITNESS

Your honor!
    (The supplication was real. The witness
    was crying.)
It was not our fault. We did not know. We had
no control. It wasn't me!
    (The scream echoes through the chamber.)

JUDGE

(To the bailiff.)
Remove him.
    (The sound of boots precedes a man
    dressed in a military uniform of gray. He
    is carrying a stick, locking the
    witnesses hands behind his back as he
    drags him screaming off the stage.)

WITNESS

    (off)
    (Screaming)
It wasn't me!!
    (Off stage, the screams of the witness
    are lessened and stop suddenly with a
    sickening thud.)

JUDGE
(Turning back to the prisoner
    nonchalantly.)
What happened?

PRISONER
The movement, the offshoot, had plans of their
own to celebrate Founders Day.

JUDGE
What were they?

PRISONER
They had…
    (Trailing off.)

JUDGE
Speak.

PRISONER
May I have a glass of water?
    (The bailiff enters with a glass of
    water. The prisoner takes a long drink.)

JUDGE
What happened then?

PRISONER
They had abducted the winner of the Elders'
Beauty Pageant. The girl who would ride the
float and at the end of the day get raped by
the dictator.

JUDGE
(haughty)
You must mean the recipient of the People's
Prize, the highest honor a young woman can
receive. To represent the population; that
blessed girl who would at the end of the
glorious celebration when we remember the
sacrifice of the founder and all he did for us
has the honor of personifying the people's
love for the state by consummating a blessed
union with the head elder.

PRISONER
Ya, her.

JUDGE
What did they do?

PRISONER
At the height of the march, when the elders
were escorted to their thrones; they struck. I
didn't know. I saw with everybody else.

JUDGE
Speak.
(The judge growled.)

PRISONER
They had abducted that young girl. I think she
must have been fifteen years old. She had
strawberry blond hair and a peppering of
freckles high on her cheeks. She was thin and
beautiful and they… had… tortured… her…

                           JUDGE
Yes, *you* did.
          (Emphasis on you.)
What exactly happened to her?

                         PRISONER
I do not know, your honor. Honestly, I became
aware at the same moment as you. I saw the
video the same time as everybody.
          (His voice cracking while he sobs
          quietly.)

                           JUDGE
          (Silent for a moment.)
Tell us the rest.

                         PRISONER
They hacked the television. Just as the elders
sat, they showed their video.
          (Above and right of the prisoner, between
          the judge and the witness stand the
          still-shot of the video is projected.)
I'll never get that image out of my head, not
that you'll allow me to. There she was,
dressed in that blue robe, chained to a chair.
I do not know what they did to her, but as
everybody else I could see the bruises on her
delicate cheeks; the black rings surrounding
her sparking green eyes, and the cuts over her
once perfect body. Her strawberry hair was
gone, shaved and there were scabs on her head
where the razor had cut too deep. Around her
neck hung a sign that read 'The Whore of the
State'.
          (The prisoner shutters to a stop.)

JUDGE
Were there any voices?

PRISONER
     (rasping)
Yes there were voices, you heard them just as
I did – Founder's Day is mandatory. You would
have seen them. Everybody saw them. We all
did, every one of us…
     (Tears streaming down his face.)

     (Silence for a moment.)
The voice said 'For the women who choose the
life of a prostitute, who compete to be the
elders' playthings, rejecting the freedom
offered by September Seventh; to them and all
of their kind awaits this and worse.' And the
screen went dark, but not before a scream
filled every house in the land. I heard them
all, I still hear them all.

JUDGE
Did you recognize any of the voices?

PRISONER
     (Tears still glistening on his cheeks,
     though he has stopped crying.)
No, your honor. Ask your star witness.
     (Spitting the word star.)
He should know.

JUDGE
We have.
     (Her voice is deep and sober.)
What happened to the girl?

PRISONER
I don't know.

JUDGE
What did you do then?

PRISONER
The next morning I walked to the closest
police station and turned myself in.

JUDGE
Do you continue to plead not guilty?

PRISONER
Yes, that is my plea.

JUDGE
Even though you admit that September Seventh
did this?

PRISONER
Yes.

JUDGE
How can that possibly be?
    (The judge sounds genuinely baffled.)

PRISONER
    (Stepping down from the defendant's box
    to pace between the judge and the witness
    stand.)
Let me tell you how that can be. I am not
guilty because the violence did not come from
September Seventh. Guilt, your honor, is
living outside common law; that established
and accepted code under which the laws are

written, the court cases enacted and the police raids authorized. That sub-group of September Seventh, though I do not condone their actions, was well within the rules set in place by the state and your precious elders. The violence comes from you.

    (The prisoner raises his finger to point at the judge, both hands rising in unison because of the handcuffs.)

For all our lives all we have known is the violence. The police raid our houses, the jailers torture our leaders, the judges rule against us and throw us into dark holes filled with pain. The party's thugs find our meetings and fall upon us until we are all unconscious. We are found guilty for thinking as we choose, acting as we please, for not following a social contract that none of us has seen, much less signed. Money is illegal, and that which we are able to find we hide as if it were a crime to hold; because it is. We are forced to play the jobs lottery and work at jobs not of our choosing for products not of our liking. We are told who we should marry, how we should name our children; and at seven years old we must turn our children over to the state on threat of prison or worse. We are not guilty because the violence is such a part of our world that even the grand plan of September Seventh, written in candlelight upon stolen paper, even that treatise preached violence over others. Perhaps not the same type or grade, but the state that September Seventh envisioned varied only in degrees to that of the elders. Use of government power to engineer, to coerce, to direct and manipulate.

Sure, we thought we would do it for a better
cause, with right on our side. Isn't that
always the case? No, we are not guilty because
we juxtaposed force over force.
        (The prisoner turns to the picture of the
        girl, frozen above court.)
Even the young girl, yes we tortured her —
I'll accept the responsibility even if I did
not participate in the act. But let us not
pretend that the Elders Pageant is anything
more than rape and slavery. For all the
elegant dresses and festivities, she was just
another victim of the violence of your perfect
order. The violence is all we have ever known,
your honor. So we are not guilty if we take
the example from the state, playing within
their new, horrible common law to seek our
freedom. This one thing I have learned in
prison; I am not guilty, your honor, because I
am just like you.

                (BLACKOUT)

                (END OF SCENE)

Scene 3

SETTING: The next day. The prisoner is
wearing an elegant suit, his hair is clean and
cut nicely. The judge's dress is shabbier, she
has rings under her eyes and is missing her
hat. Her hair is messed. The warden is a
corpulent man with an evil sneer. He is bald
and wearing his uniform.

AT RISE: The prisoner is standing at his
dais. The judge is slumped over with the gavel
held limply in her hand.

                    JUDGE
          (exhausted)
Hear ye, hear ye, the court is now in session,
hearing the case of the state against Prisoner
#28957. I call our third and final witness,
the warden of the prison where the prisoner
waited for the elders' perfect justice.
          (Enter the warden right, striding
          confidently to assume the witness stand.)

                    WARDEN
Thank you your honor. I am pleased and honored
to be here.

                    JUDGE
What is your accusation against the prisoner?

WARDEN
I accuse him of the worst offense of all, of
thought crimes. He has denied the perfect
order, the deity of the founder and the
legitimacy of the elders. He has made
statements that are interdict, and said words
that are forbidden.

JUDGE
How do you know this?

WARDEN
I watched him this long time. I listened to
his conversations. He is, naturally, a
prisoner of some consequence. And, when he was
to be brought here, we searched his cell and
found this.
          (The warden holds up the ream of paper
          from the meadows in its plastic wrapping,
          now filled with line after line written
          in tiny cursive lettering.)

JUDGE
What is in it?

WARDEN
A confession.

JUDGE
Make your case.

WARDEN
Prisoner, how do you plead?

PRISONER
Guilty, as charged.

                    WARDEN
          (Waving the ream in the air like a
          trophy.)
You do not deny that this is yours?

                   PRISONER
No, that is mine.

                    WARDEN
When did you write this?

                   PRISONER
That is a document started in the meadows and
which has grown over the years as we refined
our thoughts and our understanding.

                    WARDEN
How did you get it into my prison? I said how?

                   PRISONER
          (The prisoner shrugs and smiles sadly.)
A voice brought it to me.

                    WARDEN
It is of no consequence. We will find out
later. Your honor, let me read you a few
passages from this abomination.

                    JUDGE
No. The prisoner has pleaded guilty. I will
not have my courtroom used as a platform for
treasonous ideas. Submit the papers as
evidence and leave them.

                        WARDEN
Yes your honor.
        (Sounding disappointed.)
Prisoner, you admit that you were involved in
thought crimes.

                       PRISONER
I have pleaded guilty, though I don't
recognize the crime.

                        WARDEN
        (The warden speaks as he walks across the
        distance to deposit the papers in front
        of the judge.)
Tell the court, please, why you have pleaded
guilty to this charge when you deny your
responsibility to the other charges.

                       PRISONER
Because, in this case, I truly have defied the
elders. In this case, I have been involved in
anti-state activity. This time, my actions are
not in line with what I have learned from my
overlords, but for myself alone.

                        WARDEN
I will ask then for your confession. What are
the crimes you have committed, and why are you
guilty?

                       PRISONER
I am guilty because I believe I am equal to
all of you, even the founder and the elders.
We are the same. This, of course, to you is
treason. From the time we are born, we are
told of the omnipotence of the elders and the

deity of the founder. It is communicated with
such conviction that it defies even
discussion. For many years I did not object,
despite my hatred for the actions of the
state. Then, during one of the mandatory
broadcasts that the elders held to deliver
their messages and inform us of how we would
behave, I saw something that changed
everything. One of the elders, the old one,
was standing to gesture at a map when he
slipped, scraping his arm on the corner of the
table. The scrape was deep and a small droplet
of blood splashed onto his snow white tunic;
and he cursed quietly before regaining
composure. I do not know if others saw this;
but for me it was transformational.
    (An outburst of murmuring from the
    court.)
The elders bleed, and curse.
    (The judge's gavel comes down hard.)
They are just like me. That simple act has led
me in a direct line to now, standing here
before you, not as an inferior or a subject
but as an equal.

                    JUDGE
    (In panic.)
ORDER, ORDER I SAY.
    (Pounding her gavel over and over.)

                    WARDEN
    (Screaming above the voices, which slowly
    die down.)
You are mistaken. What you saw never happened.

JUDGE
(Regaining some composure.)
Strike that testimony from the record.

PRISONER
(calm)
As you wish. You may deny; it is of no
consequence. I know the truth.

WARDEN
And you will die with it.
(Immediately swallowing his words.)

JUDGE
Is there anything else?

PRISONER
Yes, your honor. There is more. I am guilty
because I tried to live an unsupervised life.
From the very beginning the state is our
constant companion through life. Babies are
brought back to homes that are wired. Our most
intimate conversations recorded. The anonymous
minders watch as we suffer through disease,
infertility, addiction, marital strife and
poverty. We are a reality show for the
enjoyment of our betters. We fornicate for
their pleasure, we fight to provide them
entertainment; we live our lives conscious of
their constant vigilance, which distorts the
very fabric of our relationships and
interactions. The cameras - everywhere the
cameras. On the street corners, from the
television sets, in the public and private
bathrooms. Flying above our heads in
dirigibles and attached to the dogs that run

wild through the streets; it was the cameras
that initially drove me to dissent. Living
under the watchful eye of the anonymous drove
me mad. I found a place with no cameras where
a group of people - people I chose, my people
- broke this supervision; at least for limited
moments. We made love under the stars to
people of our choosing, we sang songs of
freedom that we wrote, by ourselves; we read
poetry and short stories. We exchanged clothes
for the pleasure of donning something not
destined for us by the planners; or we went
naked as the greatest act of self-ownership. I
am guilty because I said no to the
supervision; and I am here because I was not
strong enough.

WARDEN
Is that all, prisoner?

PRISONER
    (Stepping down from the dais to face the
    audience.)
By no means, sir. I am also guilty because I
sought to think for myself, to know truth as
only an individual can know it. This is no
mean feat in a land where everything is
official. Our books are written by the
government and screened by the censors; our
television shows only give regurgitated half-
truths or outright lies. We are denied any
footing upon which to stand firm and judge the
world around us. We are told this is not our
place or our right. 'Everything is already
known' our teachers say. 'The perfect order
has all the answers, if only we would just

follow them.' To assure this is never challenged, paper is registered and carefully controlled, pens and pencils are provided by the state and include tracking chips and wireless technology to transmit back to the minders each word written; although those are easily fooled, as we have learned. Algorithms are used to screen conversations for patterns of words which could be subversive. The stranglehold is complete; parents are afraid of children lest they be called out during an adolescent outburst. Children are afraid of parents who might be forced to choose between their own lives or the lives of their young.

 (Raising his manacled hands together as a demonstration.)

We chose to break this. At the meadows, we triangulated our information, trying to cut through the double speak to get at truth. We talked about rumors – even the word is forbidden and has been struck from the dictionary. We had to teach it to our new converts, along with the word liberty; yes your honor I said it again: freedom. We relived moments of consequence from different perspectives and juxtaposed them against the official versions. And we shared what we knew of the outside world. Sporadic information; a slipped word there, a letter here, a movie that made it through or a radio program before it was jammed – all this we assembled to try to make sense of the madness. Of this I am guilty.

WARDEN
Have you finished?
     (Trying to look bored)

PRISONER
     (Still standing facing the audience.)
I have just one more thing to say - one more
crime to which I will admit. I am guilty
because I choose not to be a slave. From the
moment we are born we are told that we exist
to serve others. Never are we explained who
these mysterious others are, or why we should
exist in bondage to them. And never, ever are
we told that the true purpose of the bondage
is not to provide milk to our neighbors or
heating to a stranger, but to provide luxury
to the party members. This is the master plan
that remains unwritten and unsaid; but is at
the heart of our slavery. We are taken from
our families at the age of seven, unless we
are lucky enough to be born into the party; we
are tested at thirteen and placed in our work
camps at sixteen, unless we show extraordinary
ability in which case we are sent to further
our skills to provide greater service to our
masters through the Founders Fellowships. We
produce what their massive matrices dictate
from their laboratories of central planning.
All the basic needs of the permanent majority
- the permanent majority poor, a fact they
never tell us, kept poor to perpetuate our
slavery, and your luxury - are recorded in
massive spreadsheets managed by the Institute
of National Consumption and filled with the
daily data of national production. Never are
we to decide where we want to work, what we

want to do with the fruits of our labor. We
are told this is selfish, and selfishness is
of course evil.
        (Shaking his handcuffs.)
I am guilty because I said no to this. We in
September Seventh rejected this too. We
devised a plan. We went on strike. Not an
obvious strike which would land us in jail; a
clandestine strike. Wherever we worked, we
sought to interrupt the production. We broke
machinery, we ruined food and materials, we
fomented anger in the minds of our co-workers,
we urinated in the milk, we defecated in the
bread dough, we broke light bulbs and
installed viruses in computers. Those who went
to university failed one test after another.
Answers became gibberish, nobody studied.
School books were lost, and others destroyed.
Paper distributions were sabotaged, fire
engulfed the libraries. For every job we were
assigned to, it took two or three to clean up
the mess. At the meadows we had sex with those
we loved to produce children unwanted by the
state; mixed race children, children of
inferior genetics. Love children. I am guilty
of making life miserable for my masters. I did
this not for the fun of sabotage, like you
have always said. I did this because it was
the only way to walk upright. Each time, I
dreamed of a different life. To do what I
love, to live where I wished, to marry who I
wanted, to read what filled my soul with
wonder - to engage in freedom - yes I said it
again - to engage in freedom with others. That
is why we resisted.

                    JUDGE
     (Looking up from a newspaper she was
     reading, dated to the following day and
     with the word "GUILTY" in bold letters
     upon it, as she pretended to ignore his
     admission.)
That is quite a list.

                   WARDEN
I think we've heard enough.

                    JUDGE
Are you finished?

                  PRISONER
I am.

                   WARDEN
Your honor, I believe that the state has made
its case.

                    JUDGE
Before I rule.
     (The judge leaned forward, her labored
     breathing a rasping that cut directly and
     intimately to the prisoner who still
     stands before her. A dark pall covers the
     court, emanating somehow from the judge.)
I want to tell you something. It may come as a
surprise, it may not. But the truth is
everything to which you have confessed – the
state knew. We recorded your activities in the
meadows; often laughing at your antics. We
listened to your conversations, we knew your
plans, we heard your conspiring, and we mocked
your nudity and recreational sex. Even in your

most free - yes, I am allowing myself to use
that word, because it holds no meaning - you
were under our control. We followed your
pattern of sabotage, we met with each of your
new recruits, and we waited. We waited for the
right time, when we would obtain the maximum
impact from your treason; to destroy you and
yours once and for always. Even in your petty
resistance, you were a pawn of the state. That
is our secret, but one I want you to know as
you go.

                    PRISONER
        (Looking crestfallen, he staggers to sit
         on a corner of the witness stand.)
But, if so, why—?

                     JUDGE
Never ask why. The state has its own reasons.
We used you when we needed to, allowed you to
behave as you pleased for as long as it suited
us. To be sure, the murder of the pageant
winner caught us by surprise; but even that
served our purpose. In your moments of
greatest freedom, you were still a tool of the
state. Your whole life has not only been
futile, but was part of a larger plan by the
elders to extend the Perfect Order.
Incidentally they wanted me to tell you 'Thank
You'.
        (The prisoner sits with his head in his
         hands.)
Now, back to the issue at hand. You have had a
chance to hear the case against you. Do you
have any last words?

PRISONER
(Crying, but not weeping, tears
glistening on his cheeks, the prisoner
stands. He turns to square his shoulders,
not drying his eyes, and he lifts his
head to stare the judge full in the eyes.
As he composes himself, the judge seems
to shrink away.)
Yes your honor, only a precious few. I want to
tell you that you did not win, as you believe,
because despite having been born defeated, I
still dreamed.

JUDGE
Prisoner #28957, I find you—

(BLACKOUT)

(END OF SCENE)

Scene 4

SETTING: A different prison. The walls are
made of crumbling cement cinderblocks. There
is a large window with rusted metal bars that
looks out over a barren cold valley. In the
distance, framed at the center of the window
sits a snow-covered mountain range. Through
the window can be seen a bombed out,
devastated city. Three story buildings with
walls missing, piles of rebar and cement and
large holes in the road as if from scatter
munitions or barrel bombs. Patrolling the
streets in green jeeps are soldiers in crisp
grey uniforms under stoic visages. A red flag
new and bright displaying the hammer and cycle
is flying above the destroyed town. Inside the
prison room is a bucket with water, and
another. A rusted metal cot with stains on it
sits to one side.

AT RISE: The cell is inhabited by a middle-
aged man. He has the tan-burned skin of
somebody used to harsh cold weather and high
altitudes, and an angry stare in eyes that are
a witness to ancient Himalayan heritage. He is
wearing a frayed button down shirt thin and
torn and missing several buttons over jeans
which too have holes in the knees. They are
too big, and no belt holds them up, so they
sag. His feet are bare. He has a graying five-
o'clock shadow and salt-and pepper sprinkled
black hair. In his hand, clutched close to his
chest, is a book. He is standing on an orange
plastic chair, with a homemade noose of white

rope around his neck, hung from one of the
metal ceiling supports.

                    VOICE
          (A clear bass voice booms around the
           cell, and the man looks to his left.)
You know you're never gonna get out of here.
Not even like that.

                  (CURTAIN)